TOO MUCH SNOW ...

Dear Diary,

This is probably the very worst day of my
life. All I want is to be a Very Noble Knight.
and I thought it was REALLY going to
happen because I only have two more tasks
to do - but it's snowing! And Aunt Egg
says Prune and I can't go outside, so I'm
stuck here in Mothscale Castle until the
sun comes out again. It's boring boring
BORING ... and I wish Mother and Father
had never sent me to stay here. It's
freezing cold because Aunt Egg's
too mean to light the fires until teatime,

and there's nothing to do. Even the wolves in the forest didn't howl last night – I expect they're all curled up in a nice cosy den. Wish I was in a nice cosy den.

It's SO annoying, because I've done four of the tasks I need to do to be made a knight. I've got my True Companion (my cousin Prune), my snow-white steed (Dora), my sword, and my shield. The magic scroll is hidden under the hay in Aunt Egg's stables (she doesn't know) all ready to tell me and Prune what our next task is ... and we can't leave the castle!

Sam pushed his pen away, and stared out of his bedroom window. Outside, the snowflakes

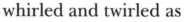

whirled and twirled as if they were never going to stop, and he sighed a huge sigh.

"Dandy," he said, "what do you think'll happen if we can't do the fifth task today? Will it stop me getting to be a Very Noble Knight?"

The doodlebird put his head on one side. "AWK," he said, "AWK."

"Really?" Sam brightened. "We should read the scroll anyway?"

The doodlebird nodded. "Awk."

"Even though we can't go outside?"

The doodlebird nodded more emphatically.
"Awk!"

Sam jumped up. "I'll go
and find Prune." He hurtled
out of his room and leapt
down the tower stairs.

The doodlebird flew after him, and the
two of them arrived at the bottom in such a
rush that Uncle Archibald, who was coming
out of his study with a pile of books, had to
skip sideways to avoid being flattened. The
books went flying, and Sam skidded to a halt.
"Ooops! Sorry, Uncle Archie." As he began to
pick up the scattered books a title caught his
eye, and he stopped to look at it. "Hey! This is
all about knights! And armour!"

Uncle Archie went pale. "Ssssh!"

Sam didn't hear him. He had opened the book. "I say, Uncle Archie! This is REALLY interesting! It's got all the names for the different bits of armour ..."

His uncle was jigging from foot to foot in extreme agitation. "Yes, yes ... now, do be a good chap, and stop reading.

Can't have your aunt upset, what what what? Hates it all, don't you know … no time for the past. Wants all my books gone. Burnt." He turned a guilty shade of puce. "Told her I'd done it … but couldn't quite do it at the time."

"So where were you going with them?" Sam asked.

Uncle Archie shook his head, and sighed a gusty sigh. "Kitchen stove. Has to be done. All clear today. Cook's having her rest, and your aunt's feeding the beasts. Prunella's helping her."

Sam was horrified. "But you mustn't burn them! Isn't there somewhere you could hide them? A cellar, or something?"

A thoughtful expression came over Uncle Archibald's face. "The cellar, eh? … Had almost forgotten about the cellar. Not been there for years! Not allowed down the stairs,

of course. Especially on Tuesdays." The old
man sighed again. "Your Aunt Eglantine
– wonderful woman, of course – made me
promise. But there's a cupboard near the top
… should be big enough." He gave Sam a slap
on the back that sent him reeling. "Good lad!
Good lad! Not a word to
your aunt,
mind. Word
of honour?"

Sam looked at his uncle with interest. When he had first come to stay at Mothscale Castle he had thought that Uncle Archie was both mad and scary. Gradually, however, he had become fond of him – and when he discovered that his uncle had once been a Very Noble Knight, he was thrilled. He longed to hear exciting stories of Knightly Deeds – but there was a problem.

Any mention of armour, tournaments, swords or shields made Aunt Egg so furious she turned purple – and nobody in Mothscale Castle wanted a furious Aunt Egg, particularly Sam. She was not the easiest of aunts even when cheerful; when angry, she was terrifying.

Now, however, it seemed that he had formed an alliance with Uncle Archibald – and who knew what he might learn? He held out his hand. "I won't breathe a word. You have the word of Sam J. Butterbiggins."

z zz

"Good lad …" Uncle Archibald coughed as he shook Sam's hand. "Ahem." He gave a nervous glance over his shoulder, and bent down to Sam's level. "Interested in knights, what?"

"Oh YES," Sam breathed.

Uncle Archibald winked, and his moustache tickled Sam's ear. "Thought as much. Bit bored today? Can't get out?"

Sam nodded, wondering what was coming next.

"Have a look at the cellar yourself." Uncle

Archie coughed again. "Ahem. Take Prune. Be glad to get away from her mother, I'd say. Beasts playing up – terrible noise! Your aunt's not happy … not happy at all. One or two things down there from the old days, don't you know." A wistful tone came into his voice. "Best days of my life, the old days …"

"They must have been VERY interesting," Sam said. "I'd love to hear all about them—"

"Harrumph!" His uncle gave an embarrassed snort. "Shouldn't have said that about the old days. No no no … not at all. Be obliged if you'd forget it, dear boy."

"Of course," Sam promised.

"Much obliged." Uncle Archibald patted Sam on the head. "But you and Prune might care to take a look. Wednesday today, so quite safe. Not sure what you'll find – but better than hanging around with nothing to do."

Sam's eyes shone, and he beamed at his uncle. "Thank you VERY much," he said, and Uncle Archibald put his finger to his lips.

"Not a word to Aunt Egg, mind. Not a word! Harrumph!" And he stalked away, the pile of books clutched to his chest.

Sam looked after his uncle for a moment. "He looks lonely," he thought. "It's a shame he can't talk to anyone about the old days. Poor old Uncle Archie."

THE FIFTH TASK

"Woooeee! Uncle Archie's my friend!" Sam was smiling as he and the doodlebird hurried towards the wing of the castle where Aunt Egg offered Luxury Holiday Accommodation for Regal Beasts. As he came nearer he could hear variously assorted roaring, screeching and growling noises.

"Prunella!" His aunt's booming voice made him jump. "Prunella – will you PLEASE hurry up! The wyverns have been waiting MUCH too long! Just listen to that miserable howling!"

Sam grinned, and let himself in through the arched doorway. His aunt was frowning at his cousin, and Prune was scowling back at her. "I've fed them, Ma, and they're howling more than ever."

Aunt Egg's frown deepened. "I can't imagine why they're so upset." She went to inspect the wyverns, and came back shaking her head. "They haven't touched their bikkies … oh dear, oh dear. Whatever will Lady Nesta say if they aren't happy? She's a new customer, and she's paying top rates … they mustn't lose weight while they're here. POOR little things! Perhaps their tummies are sore. I'll give them a spoonful of cod liver oil."

"Now I DO feel

sorry for them." Prune threw down the bag of wyvern biscuits and, as she did so, noticed Sam. "Hi, Sam! I've finished here – let's go."

"Prunella! You have not finished feeding the beasts!" Aunt Eglantine drew herself up to her full height, and gave Prune her most chilling stare. Sam quailed, but Prune took no notice.

"Yes I have. Come on, Sam." And she grabbed Sam's arm, hauling him away to where the doodlebird was waiting by the door.

As soon as they were clear of the Holiday Accommodation and back in the main hall of the castle, Sam turned to Prune. "The scroll! We've got to see what it says for today!"

Prune looked at him in surprise. "It's still snowing! Ma will chop us into little bits and feed us to the stupid wyverns if we try to ride out of here."

Sam lowered his voice, even though there was no chance of his aunt hearing him. "Dandy says we should read it, and your father says there are knightly things in the cellar we might like to look at ..."

"Pa said that?" Prune was astonished. "REALLY?"

Sam nodded. "Yes." He rubbed his nose as he remembered his conversation with his uncle. "He said something about us being safe because it's Wednesday, but it isn't, is it? It's Tuesday today."

"Of course it's Tuesday. Pa never knows what day it is," Prune told him. "Come on! What are you waiting for?" She was already heading towards the door that led to the stable yard, and Sam hurried to catch her. Together they scurried across to the stables; the yard had been swept clear of snow that morning, but the ground was white again, and heavy flakes were falling. The doodlebird flew a brief circle, then retired to the shelter of the castle.

"AWK," he remarked as he shook the snow off his feathers. "AWK!"

"Brrrrr!" Sam shivered. "It's FREEZING out here!"

Prune didn't bother to answer. She pulled the stable door open, and the two cousins slipped inside. "Hi, Weebles!" she said as her pony whickered a greeting. "We've come to see you."

"Well, we sort of have." Sam waved to his own horse, Dora, and gave Prune's pony a friendly pat. He fished under the hay in the pony's manger, and pulled out the scroll with a flourish. "Thanks, Weebles. You've kept it very safe." He turned to Prune. "Ready?"

"Ready!" Prune nodded. "Open it up!"

Sam carefully unrolled the ancient parchment as Prune leant over his shoulder. "Here we go!" he said, and Prune held her breath.

At first glance the scroll appeared empty, but one by one gleaming golden letters began to flicker into being. The letters gradually became words, and Prune read them out loud.

"'Greetings to all who wish to be Truly Noble Knights …' Yes, yes. We know all that.

Hurry up!"

"Here comes the rest," Sam said. "Look … 'For thy fifth task, thou must take thy sword and shield, and learn …' What does that next bit say?"

Prune peered more closely at the shining letters. "Erm … 'Learn the noble art of fair combat, and use thy skills against a fearsome foe. Remember that good deeds will serve thee well, and be ever gracious in triumph – ' Oh no! It's fading already … but that all sounds easy peasy. It's much easier to understand than the other tasks."

"I suppose," Sam said doubtfully. "But how do I learn the noble art of fair combat? Who's going to teach me? And where am I going to find a fearsome foe if we can't even leave the castle?"

"Don't ask me." Prune shrugged, then grinned. "Ma's pretty fearsome when she's mad about something ..." Sam's horrified expression made her snort with laughter. "I was JOKING, Sam. Besides, she wouldn't be very thrilled if you attacked her with a sword. Maybe there's something fearsome in the cellar? Let's go and find out – but you'd better fetch your sword and shield first."

Sam nodded, and made his way to Dora's stall while Prune returned the scroll to its hiding place. "Hi, Dora!" he said. "Sorry – but we're not going out today." He stroked the big white horse's nose, and she nuzzled his shoulder. "I've come to collect my Knightly Weapons."

The horse whinnied, and stood to one side. Sam squeezed past her, pulled at a loose board above her water bucket, and carefully lifted his precious sword and shield out of their hiding place. Pushing the board back, he stood up straight. "Sam J. Butterbiggins, Knight in Training!" he said. "Are you ready for the next task, True Companion?"

"Ready," Prune said. "But we've got to be careful. If Ma sees you with a sword and shield she'll go bananas. Let me go first, and if you hear me whistle – HIDE!"

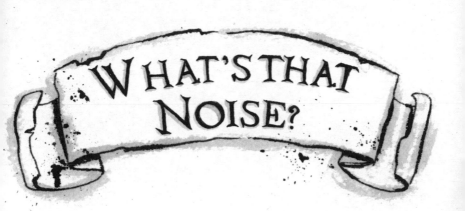

WHAT'S THAT NOISE?

Sam and Prune tiptoed their way across the icy stable yard and into the castle. Once inside, Prune went ahead while Sam and the doodlebird followed. Luck was with them, and they reached the door to the castle cellar without any sign of Aunt Egg.

"She's probably singing the wyverns to sleep," Prune said as she tried to turn the handle. "Poor old wyverns. Ma can't sing a note— hey! This door's locked! Can you see a key anywhere?"

"Maybe it's on top of the door frame?" Sam suggested. "That's where my grandmother always hides keys."

Prune squinted upwards. "You might be right … I can see something … is it a key, though?"

The doodlebird put his head on one side. "AWK?" He flew to the top of the door, picked up a large key, and dropped it down to Sam. "AwK!"

"Thanks, Dandy," Sam said, and Prune nodded.

"Good work, bird. Come on, Sam. Open the door!"

Sam put the key in the lock and, after gritting his teeth and using both hands, there was a rusty squeak and the key turned.

"Hurrah," Prune said as the door swung open. In front of them was a flight of stone steps leading downwards, while just inside the doorway was a small cupboard. "What do you think's in here?" Prune asked as she opened it. "Oh! Just a pile of old books. Boring."

"No they're not," Sam protested. "They're all about knights and armour!"

Prune stared at him. "How do you know?"

"They belong to your dad … SH!" Sam held up a hand in warning. "What's that noise?"

The cousins held their breath, and listened intently. From somewhere far below came a long plaintive wail.

"Doesn't sound at all happy," Prune said. "Do you think one of Ma's beasts has got in here by mistake?"

"I don't know." Sam shook his head. "It didn't sound much like an animal. It was ..." he hesitated. "More ghostly ..."

"Hurrah! Let's go ghost hunting!" Prune slammed the cellar door shut behind her with an enthusiastic **BANG!** Immediately, the wailing stopped, and there was complete silence.

"Oh no!" Sam looked anxious. "What if Aunt Egg heard, and she comes to see what we're doing?"

Prune snorted. "Don't be such a scaredy cat. Come on!"

It was obvious that no one had been down the stairs for a very long time. Cobwebs trailed down from the ceiling, and at every step clouds of dust flew into the air making the doodlebird cough. The light was dim; there was a small window near the door, but as the two cousins went further and further down it grew darker and darker, until Prune was forced to stop.

"I can't see a thing," she complained. "We should have brought a lantern!"

"AWK." The doodlebird left Sam's shoulder, and flapped away into the darkness. A moment later he was back, and Prune heard Sam give a startled grunt.

"What is it?" she asked.

"Dandy's found a candle," Sam told her. "Isn't he clever? He can see in the dark. It's really useful."

Prune sniffed. "A candle's not much good if we can't light it."

"AWK!" The doodlebird disappeared again. There was a pause, followed by a rattling noise.

"What's he got now?" Prune wanted to know.

"I think," Sam said, "it's a tinderbox … hang on a minute … YES!" There was a scrape and a scratch, a flurry of bright sparks, and the candle was lit. As the flame flickered into life the wailing began again, now very much nearer.

***"Ooooooooooooooooh!
Ooooooooooooooooooh!
Ooooooooooooooooooooh!"***
"AWK!" The doodlebird's feathers stood up on end, and Sam and Prune found they were holding hands.

"What is it?" Prune whispered.

Sam swallowed hard. A Knight in Training, he told himself, isn't frightened of anything.

"It's OK, Prune," he said. I'll go ahead and see what it is. You stay here—"

Prune snatched her hand back. "What? And miss all the fun? Not likely! And I wasn't scared. I was just … surprised." She paused, and listened. "It's stopped now. Maybe it was the wind blowing down the chimneys."

"I wasn't scared either," Sam lied, and he held the candle higher. "Look! There's a door at the bottom of the stairs …" His voice died away as he read the large sign hanging on the door handle.

KEEP OUT!

NO ENTRY!

DO NOT (repeat NOT) OPEN THIS DOOR!

ARCHIBALD – THIS MEANS YOU!!!

Eglantine
Duchess of Mothscale Castle

"Wow!" Prune's eyes gleamed. "Now we HAVE to see what's on the other side. Ma must have shut something belonging to Pa in there. Something she doesn't want him to have, like a suit of armour."

"Or a sword and lance," Sam agreed. "But what was making that terrible noise?"

"Let's find out," Prune said. "The key's right here in the lock," and she opened the door.

WHOOOOOOOOOSH!

A gust of wind blew out the candle, but

there was no need for it now. As Sam and
Prune stepped through the doorway they
found themselves in a vast cellar lit by
hundreds of guttering lanterns balanced
on piles of chests, barrels and boxes. An
exceptionally large suit of rusty armour was
propped in a corner, and heaps of crumbling
shields, lances, helmets and other
equipment littered the stone
floor.

"WOW,"
Prune said as
she bent to pick
up a badly dented
breast plate. "That
must have hurt—"

"Wooooooo . . .
Woooooooo . . .
Woooooooo . . . "

Sam and Prune jumped, and the doodlebird squawked. The suit of armour was clanking slowly towards them, its arms outstretched. "Hast come at last, my noble friend? Why didst thou wait so long?" The voice was as creaky and rusty as the armour.

Prune and Sam looked at each other in astonishment. "Does he mean US?" Sam asked.

"Oi! Stop! Back! Back, Sir Giles!" A small man dressed in faded red and yellow had appeared. There was a faint mistiness about him, but his voice was firm. "Not your friend, Sir Giles. Not at all. Children, Sir Giles … BACK!"

The small man herded the suit of armour into its corner, then turned to Sam and Prune. "Mustn't let him hug you. Not while he's wearing that armour! Real armour, you see – not ghostly. He'd crush you flat! Doesn't know

his own strength." He shook his head, and the bells on his hood tinkled. "Poor Sir Giles. Delighted to meet you, by the way. I'm Jingle the jester ..." And he held out his hand.

Sam, always polite, leant forward to shake it – and leapt in the air with a yell as he was sprayed with water.

"YUCK! That's COLD!" He rubbed his arms as the jester and Prune collapsed into giggles.

"Well done, Mr Jingle," Prune chortled.

"That was really funny!"

Jingle put his head on one side. "A flower for your thanks, young lady!" He snapped his fingers, a red rose dropped from the ceiling, and he presented it to Prune. "A sweet-scented rose for your delicate nose ..."

"Mmmm ..." Prune plunged her nose into the soft petals. "It smells wonder— ATCHOOOO!" And she sneezed ten times without stopping.

Sam tried to hide his smile, but the jester hooted with laughter. "Sneezy wheezy, sneezy wheezy!" he sang.

As Prune gave a half-hearted grin
the rose withered, then vanished.
"Ha ha ha," she said. "Do you play
jokes on everyone, Mr Jingle?"

The jester spun round in a circle.
"'Tis a long long time since I have
had the pleasure of doing so here in
Mothscale Castle. Since the door
was closed and locked by She Who
Does Not Smile, there's been no
call for jokes and jests." He pulled
out a large green handkerchief,
wiped his eyes, then shook the
handkerchief in front of Prune's
face. A dozen bright green
butterflies fluttered out; Prune
gasped, and Sam clapped his
admiration.

"That's BRILLIANT," he

said. "But what about Sir Giles? Doesn't he like jokes?"

"Him? Take a look …" The jester hopped and skipped his way to the enormous suit of armour. "Bend!" he ordered. Sir Giles did as he was told, and as soon as he could reach, Jingle pulled off his helmet …

… and there was nothing inside.

Or was there? Sam squinched up his eyes and stared as hard as he could. Could he see the shadow of a face, a pale mournful face with a drooping moustache? He was almost sure he could … or was he imagining it?

"See?" Jingle put the helmet back in place. "Fading away. Used to be a jolly kind of ghost, just like me, but he's worn out with loneliness. Sad. Very sad."

"But …" Sam scratched his head, his thoughts whirling. "Did you say … that is, do you mean …"

Prune gave him a superior look. "What it means, Sam," she said, "is that Sir Giles is a ghost – and so is Mr Jingle!"

Jingle winked at her, ran at the wall – and

went straight through. A moment later he was back, roaring with laughter. Prune laughed too, but Sam didn't join in.

"I'm trying to work something out," he said. "You said She Who Does Not Smile locked the door, and that must be Aunt Eglantine, so THAT means—"

There was a rattling and clanking, and Sir Giles began to shiver and shake. "Speak not that name!" He raised an arm as if to protect himself. "Speak not the name of She Who Does Not Smile!"

"She who does not— oh!" Prune's eyes opened wide. "I get it! You mean Ma!" She nudged Sam, and hissed, "That's a really good name for her!"

Sam wasn't able to say any more. Sir Giles had begun to wail, and it was impossible to be heard against the ***Wooooooooooooo!***

Woooooooooooo! Wooooooooooooos.

"Hush, Sir Giles ... hush!" Jingle soothed, "hush ..." He turned to Sam and Prune. "Could you sing a little song? Something calming, like twinkle twinkle little star?"

"Erm ..." Sam rubbed his nose while he tried to remember the words. "Erm ... yes." He did his best, and Prune joined in. Her tuneless drone was evidently just what was needed, as the wailing died gradually away.

The jester lowered his voice. "Best not mention your aunt in future, if you don't mind. Makes him anxious. He'll be quiet now, until it's time to fight the Knotted Worm."

"Fight the Knotted Worm?" Sam's face

lit up, and he put his hand on the hilt of his sword. "What's that?"

The jester shrugged. "Happens every Tuesday at four o'clock, and today's Tuesday. Old tradition … Sir Giles, Duke of Mothscale Castle, versus the Knotted Worm. One of these days Sir Giles will vanish altogether, and then the Knotted Worm will win – and who knows what'll happen then? I can't fight the worm. I'm not a knight." And Jingle sighed, and leant against a wall.

THE ART OF
FAIR COMBAT

"Duke of Mothscale Castle?" Prune turned to look at the suit of armour. "So he must be a kind of ancestor of mine. Pa is Duke of Mothscale."

The jester brightened. "Really?" He did some counting on his fingers. "I'd say ... great great great great great great grandfather. Or thereabouts."

"WOW!" Prune was impressed. "Hey, Sam! Did you hear that? We've got to help! We can't let my ... my whatever it was times great grandfather be beaten by a worm. No way!"

Sam nodded, and positioned himself in front of Sir Giles. "Excuse me, sir," he said, "but I am Sam J. Butterbiggins, knight-in-training, and this is my True Companion, Prunella. May we help?" He hesitated. "Actually, I do need a few tips on – what was it, Prune?"

"The art of fair combat," Prune said.

"That's right." Sam nodded. "Fair combat. I'm very keen to learn."

For a long moment nothing happened, but then there was the clank of armour, and Sir Giles stood up straight.

"Boy!" he said, and his voice was suddenly stronger. "Boy! Thy wish is to be a knight?"

"Oh yes PLEASE!" Sam beamed.

"A true and noble knight?"

Sam's smile grew even wider. "YES!"

"Then thou shalt watch, and learn!" Sir Giles pushed back his visor, and Sam was now certain that he could see a moustache. "Art ready?"

"Ready!" Sam pulled his sword out of its scabbard and swished it through the air. "What do I do first?"

"Hold still thy blade!" The ancient knight held up his hand. "The true knight does not smite without due cause."

Prune frowned. "But won't Sam have to chop the Knotted Worm's head off?"

Sir Giles reeled back in horror. "Sweet maid … speak not such things!"

"Why not?" Prune asked. "I thought being a knight meant biffing dragons and boffing monsters and bashing giants."

Sir Giles took his helmet off, and now his face was easy to see, although he still appeared to have no neck. "A knight must ever respect his foe," he said sternly. "The Knotted Worm is a noble beast. Such beasts do not bear sword or lance or dagger – so neither may I, or any knight worthy of the name. What child art thou to think so fiercely?"

"I'm Prune. Prunella of Mothscale Castle. Your great great something or other great granddaughter." Prune folded her arms and gave Sir Giles a chilly stare. "What's more, I'm Sam's True Companion, and the scroll says he needs to learn

about fair combat and then defeat
a fearsome foe – and if he doesn't,
then he won't get to be a noble knight. And
I'm here to see that he does, so there!"

Sam was listening anxiously. "Sh, Prune," he
began, but Sir Giles surprised him. Throwing
back his head he began to laugh, and he
laughed so long and so loudly that Sam and
Prune began to laugh too.

"A forceful maid indeed," Sir Giles chortled,
"and full of spirit! I would that I had such
a True Companion to cheer my days." He
saw Jingle droop, and put an arm round his
shoulder. "Indeed, thou dost thy best, but thou
and I are old. The maid is young, and full of
spirit."

Prune looked pleased, and elbowed Sam.
"See? You don't appreciate me."

"Yes I do," Sam said. "I just don't like it

when you're bossy."

"ME? BOSSY?" Prune was outraged. "When am I ever bossy?"

"Look!" Jingle clapped his hands to catch their attention. "Look!" And he pointed at Sir Giles. Sam and Prune looked. Not only was Sir Giles completely visible, but he was climbing out of the enormous suit of armour – and, to the cousins' astonishment, he was tall and slim, and dressed from head to foot in fine silver chain mail. On top of the chain mail he wore a white tunic, and a gold chain hung round his neck ...

Sam knew it was rude to stare, but he couldn't help himself. Too many questions were buzzing round his brain. "Erm

… excuse me for asking, Sir Giles – but why were you wearing that armour if it wasn't yours? It's MUCH too big for you."

The knight bowed to Jingle. "'Twas the jester. He had fears of losing me, and I of being lost, with no knightly friends to cheer my spirit. He encased me in ancient armour before I was gone for ever. A lad of foolish jokes, but always quick in mind."

Jingle bowed low in return. "Thank you, Sir Giles. And a delight to see you in – er – more solid form again!" He winked at Sam and Prune. "And talking of jokes, I have a riddle for you – what must always be broken before it can be used?"

Sam looked blank, but Prune giggled. "I know the answer. An egg!"

The jester spun round in a circle. "And how—"

HISSSSSSSSSS
SSSSSS

The hissing filled the cellar, and a stone slab
heaved, rocked, and fell over with a crash.

As Jingle, Sam and Prune backed hastily

away, an enormous serpent

began to slither out,

peering this way and

SSSSSSSSSSSSS
SSSSSSSS!!!!!

that through a pair of small gold spectacles.
When it saw the heap of discarded armour on
the ground it paused, and raised its eyebrows.
"Sssssir Gilessss? Sir Gilessssss?" With another slither
and a wriggle it pulled the rest of its body out,
and Sam saw that the tail was knotted. "The
Worm," he told himself, and he gripped his
sword more tightly.

"Boy – " Sir Giles was behind him. "Hold
fast thy shield, and guard thyself. The Knotted
Worm has much strength in her tail! For thy

safety, do as I do ..." And the knight stepped
forward, his sword lifted high in greeting.

"I salute thee, Worm!"

A FEARSOME FOE

Sam took a deep breath. The Knotted Worm
was very big, and very long … and her little
green eyes were not friendly. "I salute you, too,
Worm!" he echoed, and waved his sword.

The Knotted Worm reared up, and stared
at him. "Oi! What's this? A boy?"

"No mere boy, Worm." Sir Giles shook his head. "Sam J. Butterbiggins, knight-in-training."

"Butterbiggins, eh?" The Worm sniggered. "And aren't you scared, little Butterbiggins? I'm a great big horrible worm, you know. And I'm here to win! Win win WIN! That old knight's had his day. He's been getting slower and slower; every Tuesday he gets worse. No fun to fight any more. I've decided: today's the day when I'll turn him into a puff of cold air ... and then I'll live here for ever and ever. SSSSSSSSSS!"

"That shall not be so." Sir Giles was very calm. "I am the guardian of Mothscale Castle, and I say that day shall never come."

"Never," Sam said, and he hoped he sounded as calm.

"I should say so!" Prune was hopping with rage.

"This is MY castle, and I do NOT want any horrible beastly worms in MY cellar!"

The Knotted Worm sniffed loudly. "A weary old knight, a jester, a girl and a Butterbiggins? Boo! Boo! And PAH! to you all! Usual rules, Sir G? Best of three?"

Sir Giles slid his sword back into its scabbard, and picked up a shield. "I take thy challenge, Worm."

Sam nodded. "Me too … I mean, I take the challenge."

"Oooo er!" The Knotted Worm twitched her knotted tail. "See me tremble, little boy! See me quake!" She peered at Sir Giles. "You've taken off that tin suiting, I see. Suits me. All the easier to crush you to dust …" And she swirled and twisted so that her scales glittered in the candlelight.

"One moment!" Jingle was holding a long silver trumpet.

"In the true way of knightly combat … let the contest begin!" and he blew a long blast.

Prune, who had been staring at the serpent, caught Sam's arm. "Sam!" she whispered. "Watch out! She looks MEAN!"

Sam didn't have time to answer. The Knotted Worm was zig-zagging across the cellar, trying to pin Sir Giles into a corner. Each time it seemed as if she had succeeded, the knight leapt over her gleaming body, and returned to the centre of the floor. Sam, hardly daring to blink, watched every move. Gradually he realised that Sir Giles was waiting longer and longer before he jumped, so that, each time, the serpent was led nearer and nearer to the walls. Finally, he left it so long that Sam was certain he would be crushed – but at the last possible second the knight made a flying leap and the Knotted Worm crashed into the piles of junk with a deafening clatter and a furious hiss.

"One to me!" Sir Giles gasped.

The Knotted Worm snorted. "Mere luck. Let's go for round two!"

TAN TARRA!!! Jingle blew on his trumpet. "Point of honour! There shall be three minutes' resting time between each contest. Fair combat, Worm."

The Knotted Worm muttered to herself, but curled up in a corner. Sir Giles touched his toes, stretched his arms, and wiped his forehead with the edge of his tunic.

"Well done, sir!" Sam said admiringly. Sir Giles nodded his thanks, and glanced at Prune.

"Perchance the maid might give me a favour to wear in her honour? The honour of Mothscale Castle?"

Prune stared at him. "What? What sort of a favour?"

"It's like a sash, or a scarf, or a ribbon," Sam explained. "Knights carry them to bring them luck."

"Oh." Prune fished in her

pocket, and brought out an extremely grubby handkerchief. "Would this do? I used it to wipe the wyverns' noses, so it isn't very clean ..."

Sam inspected the handkerchief. "Ah. I think you'd better have mine," he said. "It's cleaner."

Prune took it, and handed it to Sir Giles. "Er ... good luck," she said.

"I thank you, gracious maid." Sir Giles bowed, and tucked the hankie into the top of his tunic.

"All settled?" the jester asked. "Right! Time for the second contest to begin!"

As he put the trumpet to his lips, the Knotted Worm hurled herself across the floor so fast that Sir Giles had no time to get ready. One swing of her knotted tail, and he was thrown backwards. A moment later he was pinned against the wall, and the Worm was chuckling a self-satisfied chuckle.

"My round, I think!" she said. "One all. Get ready to lose for ever, knight!"

Sam jumped forward, glaring at the Worm. "Just a minute! You cheated! You started before the trumpet!"

Prune was beside him. "Sam's right! That wasn't fair!"

Sir Giles was struggling to stand, rubbing his head as he did so. "In truth," he said, "the Noble Worm moved not until the jester spoke ..."

"See?" The Knotted Worm twisted herself round so her scaly nose was inches away from Sam's. "Think you're so clever, Butterbigginssss? Little knight-in-training? SSSSSSSSSSSSSS! Well, here's a challenge for you. YOU take me on!"

"No! No no, that may not be!" Sir Giles wavered his way to the centre of the room.

"The boy is yet unpractised in the art of combat!"

"Who cares," the Worm said rudely. "I won the last round, so it's my right to choose, and I choose the Butterbiggins. And if he wins — and I can tell you that he won't — I promise I'll leave here for ever and go and live with my great-aunt Susan in Killjoy Castle."

Sam stared into the Knotted Worm's mocking little eyes, his heart pitter pattering in his chest. "OK," he said and then, aware that he didn't sound very knightly, added, "I mean, I take your challenge, Worm."

"And we'll jolly well hold you to your promise." 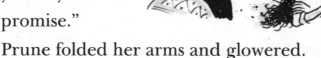 Prune folded her arms and glowered.

"That's right," Sam agreed. "If I win, you leave here for ever."

"Boy! And fair young maid!" Sir Giles was shaking his head in disapproval. "Thou must not doubt the word of a noble foe."

The Worm looked smug. "That's told YOU, young Butterbiggins. Now, get ready to lose!"

The jester picked up his trumpet, but Sam stopped him. "Please – could you just say, *One Two Three GO*?" he asked.

Jingle glanced at Sir Giles, and he nodded. The Knotted Worm rippled her gleaming scales, and Sam took a deep breath.

"One," the jester said, "two … three—" "SSSSSSSSSSSSSSSSSSSSS!!!"

The Worm scythed across the cellar at lightning speed, but Sam was expecting her.

"Wheeeee!" he shouted as he cleared the serpent's coils. At once she came slicing back, but Sam was ready, and leapt over her with inches to spare. Again and again the Worm tried to sweep him against the wall, but each time he managed to avoid defeat.

"SSSSSSSSSSSSSSSSSSS!!!" The Knotted Worm was angry. Her attacks grew more and more furious, and she began to raise her body off the floor so that Sam was forced to jump higher and higher. Then, without warning, she coiled herself into a loop and hurled herself at him, intending to flatten him once and for all. Prune shrieked, Sir Giles threw up his hands, the jester gasped –

and Sam shut his eyes, dived through the loop, and somersaulted to the other side.

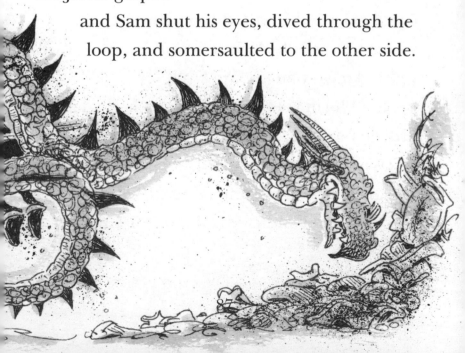

The Knotted Worm was unable to stop herself; with a mighty **CRASH!!!** she smashed into the biggest heap of barrels and chests, then lay still.

"Yes!" Prune punched the air. "Well done, Sam! You've won! You've won!"

"Indeed." Sir Giles was smiling, and Jingle was grinning from ear to ear.

Sam scrambled to his feet, dusting himself down. He was glowing with excitement, but there was something he had to do before he could glory in his win. Running over to the serpent he asked, "Knotted Worm – are you all right? Are you hurt?"

The Worm peered at him from behind a broken box. "What do you care?"

"Well ..." Sam hesitated. "Actually, I do care. I don't like hurting things. By the way, your spectacles are crooked ... excuse me."

He leant forward and straightened them.
"That's better."

"OI! SAM!" Prune put her hands on her
hips. "Honestly! What are you like? That
Worm tried to flatten you by cheating, and
now you're being NICE – "

"Hush! The boy is right." Sir Giles bent to
move the shattered box out of the serpent's
way. "A true knight is ever gracious in victory."

"And I suppose you expect me to be gracious back? Well, PAH!" the Worm snorted. "I'm not. Never have been gracious, never will be."

Prune giggled. "Maybe your great-aunt Susan will help you learn."

The Knotted Worm glowered. "SSSSSSSSS ..." And then, without another word, she slithered to the hole in the cellar floor, and disappeared.

"There she goes," Prune said cheerfully. "So ... no more Tuesday contests, Sir Giles."

The knight didn't hear her. He and the jester were pulling the stone slab back into place, and Jingle was singing merrily as they heaved and pushed. Sam went to help, but before he reached them the cellar door burst open – and Uncle Archibald came rushing in.

"Tuesday!" he gasped.
"It's Tuesday!"

"Pa!" Prune's eyes opened

wide in amazement.
"Pa! What on earth
are you doing here?"

"Prunella! My dear
girl!" Uncle Archie's hair
was standing wildly on
end. "Sam! Where's Sam?"

"Here, Uncle Archie." Sam
hurried across the cellar. "Are
you OK?"

His uncle collapsed on to a nearby barrel,
and closed his eyes. "The Knotted Worm," he
said. "I sent you into danger, what what what
... Terrible danger." His eyes opened again as
a look of terror crossed his face. "She must be
due! Any minute! Hurry! We must leave—"

"Oh, you don't need to worry about the
silly old serpent," Prune said cheerfully. "Sam
beat her hollow, and she's gone off to live with

her great-aunt Susan. She won't be bothering anyone here again, will she, Sir Giles? Erm … SIR GILES?"

Sir Giles was standing very still, staring at Uncle Archibald as if he was an apparition. Uncle Archie looked up and saw him, and for a long moment neither moved. Then, with a roar of delight, the two old men flung themselves at each other. "Giles, old boy!"

"My noble friend!"

"Woooeeee." Prune rolled her eyes at Sam. "Wonders will never cease! Fancy Pa having a friend who's a ghost!"

"I know," Sam said. "I think they used to be best friends, but Aunt Egg—"

CRASH!

The cellar door was flung open a second time, and a purple Aunt Eglantine stood fuming in the entrance, a drooping wyvern tucked under each arm.

"ARCHIBALD! PRUNELLA! SAM! I am ANGRY! VERY ANGRY! WHAT, exactly, WHAT do you mean by this behaviour?"

Uncle Archie stopped hugging Sir Giles, and began to tremble. "My – my dear," he stuttered. "The children – danger – thought it was Wednesday – realised it was

Tuesday – had to save them – didn't mean …"

"You didn't mean to disobey me?" Aunt Egg's eyes flashed, and Sam was sure he could see steam coming out of her ears. "YOU DIDN'T MEAN—"

"STOP IT, Ma! Don't be so completely and utterly HORRID!" Prune, quivering with fury, stamped her foot. "Don't you understand? Pa only came here because he thought we were in trouble. Leave him alone! You're ALWAYS bossing him about, and he was trying to help us so it's NOT FAIR! Is it, Sam?"

Sam's stomach was icy with fear, but he was determined to stand up for his uncle. "No, Aunt Egg."

Aunt Egg was, for a moment, struck dumb. She was used to Prune's attacks, but Sam had never once disobeyed her or argued with her. She was still considering how best to deal with his extraordinary behaviour when one of the wyverns gave a miserable howl. "Wowlie wowl! Wowlie wowlie! Poooooorly tumtum!"

"Hush, sweetie pie." Aunt Egg rocked it to and fro. "Auntie Eglantine's doing her best to make you better—"

"Hobbles." She was interrupted by Sir Giles, who had retreated to the darkest corner of the cellar on her arrival. "Poor beasts. A common complaint in wyverns. Hast tried green apples? 'Twill cure them."

"Cure them?" Aunt Egg's voice was sharp. "Who's that speaking? How do you know? How soon will it cure them?"

"No time at all, madam." Sir Giles turned to the jester, who was beside him. "What hast thou in thy pockets?"

Jingle twirled in a circle. "An apple a day keeps the Hobbles away," he sang, and held out a bright green apple. "Catch, dear madam!" And he tossed it across the width of the cellar.

Aunt Egg caught it, but before she had time to inspect it the two wyverns had snatched it from her. "Yum! Yum!" They broke it in half, and gulped it down with little squeaks of pleasure. A moment later they were sitting up, bright-eyed and cheery. "Weeek!" they said, "Weeek! Weeek! HAPPY tumtums!"

SHE WHO DOES
NOT SMILE

Aunt Egg heaved a huge sigh of relief, followed by an unwilling smile. "I suppose," she said, "I ought to thank you, whoever you are."

The old knight bowed from the shadows. "No need, madam."

"Yes there is!" Prune marched across the floor, dragging Sam with her. "You know what, Ma? If you want to thank Sir Giles properly you should let Pa come down here to see him."

Seeing her mother's face darken, she nudged Sam. "You tell her."

"They're ever such old friends, and they miss each other," Sam explained. "Maybe they could meet on Tuesdays?"

Aunt Eglantine didn't look much happier, and Sam searched his mind for a winning idea. "Supposing one of the other royal beasts gets ill, Aunt Egg? You could tell Uncle Archie, and then he could ask Sir Giles how to make it better."

Aunt Egg's face brightened, and she glanced towards the dark corner where Sir Giles was hiding. "So … whoever you are. You know about royal beasts, do you?"

"Blue Lurgies, Hobbles, Splayed Feet, Crossed Eyes, Noxious Plagues, Boils and Splurges. He knows about them all!" Jingle popped out from the darkness. "An expert in his field. Never known a beast not to recover in his care …"

"I see." Aunt Egg tickled the wyverns under their chins while she considered the situation. "Hmmmm … I really don't think—"

"HUH!" Prune, unable to wait any longer, heaved an angry sigh. "I knew it wasn't any good asking. You're just an old spoilsport, Ma, that's what you are. I'm not surprised they call you

She Who Does Not Smile!" She scowled at her mother, but before she could stamp away Sam caught at her arm.

"That's not fair, Prune. Give Aunt Egg a chance! You don't know what she was going to say."

"Well said, old boy. Well said!" Uncle Archie slapped Sam on the back, and there was more applause from the corner of the cellar.

Aunt Egg was looking at Prune in astonishment, mixed with horror. "'She Who Does Not Smile?'" she asked.

"That's right." Prune gave an emphatic nod. "And I can see why."

Sam, who was feeling very uncomfortable,

coughed. "But you do smile sometimes, Aunt Egg. I'm sure I've seen you smile at least … oh, at least five times!"

The Duchess of Mothscale Castle inspected him thoughtfully. "Thank you, Sam. Five times, you say? Well well well. I'll have to think about that. In the meantime, I think your suggestion is a sensible one. My beasts are very important – " here she stopped to glare at Prune – "even if SOME members of my family do not appreciate the benefits they bring. Archibald!"

Uncle Archie jumped to attention. "Yes, my dear?"

"I have made a decision. You may visit this cellar twice

a month from two o'clock until three. Any
other times must be by arrangement. And now
I must return my poochy pies to their baskets.
I shall expect to see you, Prune and Sam,
upstairs in five minutes – and there will be NO
excuses!" And Aunt Egg handed Uncle Archie
a wyvern, and steered him out of the cellar
with a firm hand.

As soon as her footsteps had died away, Sir
Giles came out of his hiding place.

"My humble thanks." He bowed to Sam,
and took the golden chain from round his
neck. Leaning forward, he
slipped it over Sam's
head. "Knight-in-
training …
thou hast learnt
the art of fair

combat, and been gracious in victory."

Sam went pink with pleasure. "Thank you! Thanks ever so much, Sir Giles."

"Hey!" Prune said. "What about me?"

Sir Giles's eyes twinkled. "In truth, fair maid, thou hast brought me back my noble friend, and for that I thank thee. But I fear you have yet to learn grace …"

Prune, totally unrepentant, giggled. "I don't suppose I ever will. I'm like the Worm. But don't worry about Pa only being allowed to come once a month. Ma's beasts are always catching something or other – Pa'll be here almost every day. But we'd better go, or Ma'll zoom back in a towering rage. Come on, Sam."

"I'm coming," Sam said. "Goodbye, Sir Giles, and goodbye, Mr Jingle. We'll see you again soon …"

Sir Giles drew his
sword, and lifted it high.
"Sam J. Butterbiggins,
knight-in-training, and
Prunella, True Companion …
I salute you both!"

WOW WOW WOW!!!! What a day! I've done my fifth task, and that means I've only got one more to do ... yippeee! And Aunt Egg didn't say ANYTHING at teatime about finding us in the cellar with all the armour and stuff ... and she smiled TWICE! Uncle Archie couldn't stop twirling his moustache. I've never seen him look so happy. But when Prune asked him why he didn't have a jester, Aunt Egg went VERY purple, and we all had to talk about the weather.

By the way, it's stopped snowing!

Join Sam and Prune
on their sixth quest!

TO THE
RESCUE!

Read on for a sneak peek ...

Hodder
Children's
Books

Dear Diary.

Oops! I'm so excited I can't write properly.
Dandy's tutting at me for being messy, but
I can't help it because today is the most
important day of my life. Today's the day
when I get to do my sixth task, and if I
get it right - TA DA!!!!

I'll be a Very Noble Knight—

CRASH!

The door to Sam's bedroom flew open, and his cousin Prune burst in.

"Sam! What are you DOING?"

Sam put his pen down. "I was just writing my diary—"

"DIARY?" Prune's expression made it very clear that she had no time for such things. "Put it away! We've got to find out what to do next. You've got your horse, and your sword, and your shield, and you've learnt your knightly skills, and" – she puffed out her chest – "you've got the best True Companion a knight-in-

training could ever have.
That's five tasks done –
and only one to do! So
let's get going!"

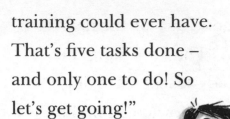

She grabbed Sam's
arm and began dragging him
towards the doorway. Sam
whistled to the doodlebird,
and the three of them
hurried down the winding
turret stairs.

"Ma and Pa have gone out for the day," Prune said cheerfully. "They're taking the hippogriff home to Lady Hacker. He only arrived yesterday, but he howled all night without stopping. Ma says she can't possibly call it Luxury Holiday Accommodation for Regal Beasts if the poor things never get a wink of sleep. She's going to give Lady Hacker her money back, and she's made poor old Pa go with her in case Lady H makes a fuss."

Sam looked surprised. "I did hear something, but I thought it was the wolves in the forest. They've been howling ever such a lot lately ... haven't you noticed?"

Prune shook her head. "No. Maybe it's a full moon. Doesn't that make them howl?"

"Could be." They were nearly at the bottom of the staircase, and Sam jumped the last three steps. "Aunt Egg says there aren't any wolves, but I'm sure I've seen some."

Prune snorted. "Ma doesn't WANT there to be wolves. Who would send their dear little pets to stay at Mothscale Castle if they thought there were horrible toothy wolves lurking nearby? She pretends they don't exist, and then she doesn't have to worry about them."

"AWK!" The doodlebird flapped his wings, and Sam laughed. "Dandy says she pretends *he* isn't here most of the time!"

"She'd probably like it if we weren't here either." Prune shook her head. "She likes the Royal Beasts much better than me."

"They don't argue with her," Sam pointed out. "You do, all the time."

His cousin giggled. "I do, don't I? Come on – let's find the scroll and see what we've got to do today!" She hopped across the hall, and opened the door that led to the stable yard. Sam followed close behind. His heart was beating fast ... what would the final task be? Would he be able to do it? What if everything went wrong?

GOBLINS

Beware - there are goblins living among us!

Within these pages lies a glimpse into their secret world. But read quickly, and speak softly, in case the goblins spot you...

A riotous, laugh-out-loud funny series for younger readers from the bestselling author of **HUGLESS DOUGLAS**, David Melling.

www.hodderchildrens.co.uk